At the BOARDWALK

by Kelly Ramsdell Fineman

Illustrated by Mónica Armiño

tiger tales

PIZZA

At the boardwalk
by the sea
Days are spent with family

Life relaxes; time is free

At the boardwalk

by the sea

At the boardwalk
  in the fog
Grab the stroller, bring the dog
Families take a morning jog

At the boardwalk
in the fog

At the boardwalk
    bubbles fly
Bumping into passersby
Salt-air breezes, kites up high
At the boardwalk
    bubbles fly

At the boardwalk
   in the sun
Take a break from beach-time fun

Ice cream cones for everyone!

At the boardwalk

in the sun

At the boardwalk
   jumbled joys
Hermit crabs and pirate toys

Arcade games make lots of noise

At the boardwalk

jumbled joys

At the boardwalk
when it rains
Grumpy gulls are weather vanes

Everyone around complains

At the boardwalk

when it rains

At the boardwalk
day or night
Treats for every appetite

Popcorn – taffy – fudge, delight
At the boardwalk
day or night

At the boardwalk
     near the sand
Sunset paints the sky and land

Shadows lengthen; stars expand

At the boardwalk

near the sand

At the boardwalk
  one last ride
Oompah music, sit astride

Carouseling, side by side

At the boardwalk

one last ride

At the boardwalk
on the pier
Music plays for all to hear

People hold their loved ones near
At the boardwalk
on the pier

At the boardwalk
day is done
Sleepy after evening fun

Strolling home – no need to run

At the boardwalk

day is done